For Daisy and Flora

First American edition published in 2002 by
Carolrhoda Books, Inc.

Copyright © 2002 by Mark Birchall

Originally published in 2002 by Andersen Press Ltd., London, England,
under the title *Rabbit's Party Surprise*.

Carolrhoda Books, Inc.
A division of Lerner Publishing Group
241 First Avenue North
Minneapolis, MN 55401 U.S.A.

Website address: www.lernerbooks.com

Library of Congress Cataloging-in-Publication Data

Birchall, Mark, 1955–
Rabbit's birthday surprise / written and illustrated by Mark Birchall. — 1st American ed.
        p.   cm.
Summary: When Rabbit's favorite doll disappears she is too sad to
enjoy her birthday party, until a bit of magic saves the day.
ISBN 0–87614–910–7 (lib. bdg.)
[1. Lost and found possessions — Fiction. 2. Toys — Fiction. 3. Parties — Fiction.
4. Birthdays — Fiction. 5. Rabbits — Fiction.] I. Title.
PZ7.B5118765 Raae 2002 [E] — dc21 2001007132

Printed and bound in Italy
1 2 3 4 5 6 – OS – 07 06 05 04 03 02

Rabbit's Birthday Surprise

Mark Birchall

❦ CAROLRHODA BOOKS, INC.

MINNEAPOLIS

Rabbit was telling Mr. Cuddles about her birthday party.

"There'll be cake with ice cream and games with prizes," she said. "I hope you'll be coming."

Mr. Cuddles didn't say a word, but Rabbit knew that he'd be there.

"Come on, it's time to go shopping for your party,"
said Mom. "There's lots to get and I'll need your help."
So off they went—Mom, Rabbit, and Mr. Cuddles.

They bought balloons and paper hats, pretzels and
juice, a sticky carrot cake . . .

. . . and much, much more!

"That must be everything," said Rabbit happily.

"Not quite," Mom told her. "There's still one more place we need to go."

And they went to hire the magician, The Amazing Ali Gator.

"Oooh, I love magic," said Rabbit. "I can't wait for the show!"

The Amazing Ali Gator gave her a poster of himself looking most impressive.

Rabbit proudly carried it home.

She helped Mom with the decorations.
At last, everything was done.

The doorbell rang.

"Your friends are here," called Mom.

"Now the party can begin."

"But I can't find Mr. Cuddles," Rabbit cried.

"Where did you see him last?" asked Mom.

"I can't remember."

"Well, where have you looked?"

"Everywhere!"

"Never mind," said Mom. "We don't have time to look now. I'm sure we'll find him later."

But Rabbit didn't want to have a birthday party without Mr. Cuddles.

She didn't want to play pin-the-tail-on-the-donkey
or hide-and-seek.

But she couldn't help peeking when The Amazing
Ali Gator showed off his card tricks.

Or when he made Miss Flamingo disappear . . .

... then reappear in a different place altogether! Rabbit's friends cheered and clapped.

The Amazing Ali Gator bowed then gave his hat a tap with his magic wand. And abracadabra–

"Mr. Cuddles!" gasped Rabbit. "I *knew* you wouldn't miss my birthday party!"

Everybody clapped again, but this time Rabbit clapped loudest of all.

"Hip, hip hooray for
The Amazing Mister Ali Gator and
Mr. Cuddles!" cheered Rabbit.
"Happy birthday, Rabbit!" shouted
all of Rabbit's friends.